KANSAS

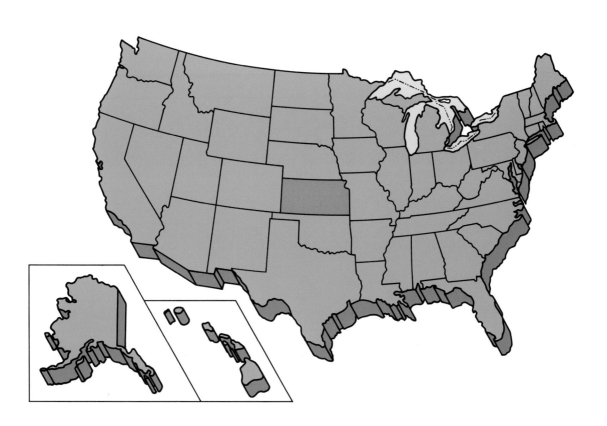

KANSAS

Charles Fredeen

Lerner Publications Company

This book is available in two editions:
Library binding by Lerner Publications Company
Soft cover by First Avenue Editions, 1997.
241 First Avenue North
Minneapolis, MN 55401
ISBN: 0-8225-2716-2 (lib. bdg.)
ISBN: 0-8225-9781-0 (pbk.)

LIBRARY OF CONGRESS
CATALOGING-IN-PUBLICATION DATA
Fredeen, Charles.
    Kansas / Charles Fredeen.
      p.   cm. − (Hello USA)
    Includes index.
    Summary: Introduces the geography, history,
people, industries, and other highlights of
Kansas.
    ISBN 0-8225-2716-2 (lib. bdg.)
    1. Kansas−Juvenile literature.
[1. Kansas.] I. Title. II. Series.
F681.3.F74 1992
978.1−dc20   91-14443

Cover photograph by Darrell
Sampson, © 1992.

The glossary that begins on
page 68 gives definitions of
words shown in **bold type** in
the text.

 This book is printed
on acid-free, recycla-
ble paper.

CONTENTS

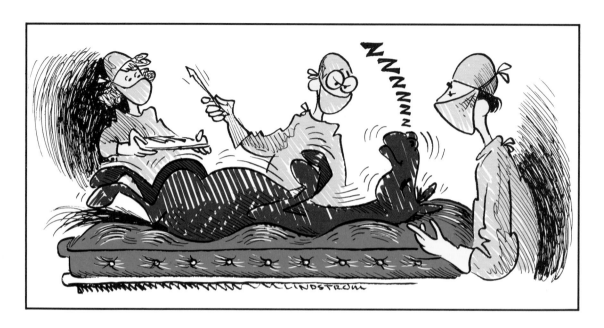

Did You Know . . . ?

☐ At the Kansas State University College of Veterinary Medicine, doctors use waterbeds as operating tables for horses.

☐ Dodge City, Kansas, is one of the windiest cities in the United States. Wind speeds average 14 miles (22.5 kilometers) per hour.

❑ The exact geographic center of the mainland United States is located in Kansas, near the town of Lebanon. For this reason, Kansas is sometimes called the Navel of the Nation.

❑ Kansas claims the world's largest salt deposit. A mine in Hutchinson is large enough to supply the United States with salt for the next 375,000 years.

❑ The world's largest meteorite, a mass of rock and metal from outer space, landed near what is now Greensburg, Kansas, about 2,000 years ago. The meteorite weighed 1,000 pounds (454 kilograms).

A brick structure marks the geographic center of the mainland United States.

7

A Trip
Around the State

Plains overflowing with tall prairie grass as far as the eye can see. Fields bursting with big yellow sunflowers. Blue skies sometimes darkened by a twister or a blinding dust storm. All of this, and much more, is Kansas.

Wheat kernels, or seeds, are ground into flour, which is used to make bread and other food products.

Kansas is a midwestern state. It sits exactly in the center of the U.S. mainland. Shaped like a rectangle, Kansas borders Nebraska, Missouri, Oklahoma, and Colorado. Kansas is known as the Breadbasket of America—that is, the major provider of wheat, one of the nation's most important foods.

Much of the state's wheat is grown in the Great Plains region, which stretches across western Kansas. Most of the Great Plains look flat, but the region actually slopes upward toward Colorado. The region reaches its greatest height in the west, at a place called Mount Sunflower. Mount Sunflower, which is not actually a mountain peak but a small hill, is 4,039 feet (1,231 meters) above sea level.

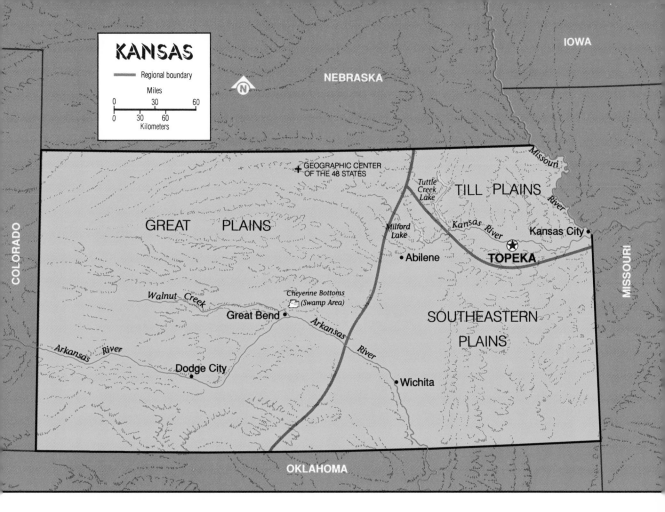

KANSAS

Regional boundary

Miles
0   30   60

Kilometers
0   30   60

NEBRASKA

IOWA

COLORADO

+ GEOGRAPHIC CENTER OF THE 48 STATES

GREAT   PLAINS

Tuttle Creek Lake

TILL PLAINS

Milford Lake

Missouri River

Kansas River

Kansas City

TOPEKA

• Abilene

Walnut   Creek

Cheyenne Bottoms (Swamp Area)

SOUTHEASTERN

Great Bend •

Arkansas   River

PLAINS

Arkansas   River

• Dodge City

• Wichita

MISSOURI

OKLAHOMA

11

Striking landforms can be seen at Monument Rocks in western Kansas. Many fossils are buried deep within the rocks.

Asters bloom throughout Kansas.

Eastern Kansas is divided into two geographic regions—the Till Plains and the Southeastern Plains. **Glaciers,** huge sheets of ice formed in prehistoric times, slowly carved through northeastern Kansas to create the region known as the Till Plains. The glaciers left deposits of **till,** or crushed rocks and dirt, which formed a rich soil. Thousands of years ago, strong dust storms carried some of this soil westward, enriching the Great Plains.

The Southeastern Plains covers southeastern Kansas. The area has **prairies** (grasslands), rolling hills, flatlands, limestone ridges, and pockets of dense forest. Farmers have taken advantage of the flatlands in the region by covering them with crops. A tall, reddish brown grass called bluestem waves gently in the wind over large sections of the Southeastern Plains. Cows and sheep graze on this grass.

Three major rivers flow through the state. They are the Kansas (also known as the Kaw), the Missouri, and the Arkansas. The Kansas River flows eastward and eventually empties into the Missouri River, which forms part of the northeastern border of the state. The Arkansas River winds through southern Kansas. Parts of the river dry up for most of the year because people use so much of its water.

Most of the large lakes in Kansas are artificial. These lakes, called **reservoirs,** were created when dams were built to store river water. The reservoirs have become popular for boating, swimming, and other water sports. Milford and Tuttle Creek are among the biggest reservoirs in Kansas.

The state's weather varies widely from season to season. During the summer, temperatures average 74° F (23° C) but sometimes pass 100° F (38° C). Winter temperatures, on the other hand, average about 30° F (–1° C) and have dropped below 0° F (–18° C).

Kansas receives about 27 inches (69 centimeters) of rain and snow each year, with the most falling on the Southeastern Plains. Throughout Kansas, winter blizzards, spring tornadoes, and summer thunderstorms and dust storms can appear suddenly, threatening the landscape. Occasionally, mild earthquakes shake the ground.

Summer storm clouds fill the Kansas sky *(above).* **After a winter storm** *(inset),* **the branches of a bush hang heavy with ice.**

Droughts, or long periods of little or no rainfall, also occur in Kansas. Droughts leave crops thirsty for water. They also leave the soil dry and loose for the wind to pick up and shoot across the plains in blinding clouds of dust.

Shade is hard to find in Kansas. Few forests shelter the land because trees, which need a lot of water, have not survived the state's frequent droughts. Only about 3 percent of the state is forestland. But several kinds of trees, such as cottonwood, maple, ash, pecan, willow, and black walnut, grow in Kansas.

Prairie grasses

More than 200 types of grasses blanket the prairies of Kansas. These kinds of plants fed the millions of buffalo that once thundered across the Great Plains. Most of the buffalo were killed for their hides or for sport in the 1800s. Only about 300 buffalo now live in Kansas and all are located on game preserves, where the animals are protected from hunters.

The most common wild animals in Kansas include pheasants, coyotes, white-tailed deer, and foxes. Scurrying prairie dogs burrow into the ground, while rabbits hop through the grasses.

Ring-necked pheasant

17

Kansas's Story

Kansas's history is filled with tales of fierce battles, shifty lawmakers, gunfights, and murder. For a time, the state was even known as Bleeding Kansas. Much of the trouble took place after the arrival of white settlers. But the state's history goes back a long way—long before Kansas even got its name.

About 10,000 years ago, Native Americans came to the central part of North America, an area that includes the land now called Kansas. These prehistoric Indians were hunters. They also ate roots and plant foods. By A.D. 1000, the Indians began planting and harvesting crops. Eventually, the tribes in the region became known as the Plains Indians.

One Plains Indian tribe was the Kaw, or Kansa. Their name means "people of the south wind." The state of Kansas was named after the Kaw.

The Kaw lived along a river now called the Kansas. They built earthen lodges, or homes, which were owned by the women of the group. Kaw women also took charge of sacred burials and oversaw the farming.

The Plains Indians, including the Kaw *(far right)*, lived in villages and farmed the land. Some tribes built houses *(below)* of earth or straw and made pots *(right)* from clay.

19

Kaw men were the hunters. The Kaw used bows and arrows to kill buffalo, their main target. The entire animal was used. The meat was eaten, and the hide became clothing and blankets for the Kaw people. They carved the bones and horns into tools and jewelry.

The Osage, another Plains Indian tribe, lived in southeastern Kansas, where game was plentiful. Thousands of buffalo grazed on the area's bluestem grasses. The Pawnee Indians lived in earthen lodges along the Arkansas River. They were highly skilled farmers. The Wichita also lived along the Arkansas River, but their homes were made of grass.

Each tribe had its own customs, but the tribes also shared many traditions. Most of the Plains Indians farmed and hunted. Warriors often belonged to military groups. All the tribes held ceremonies in which they asked their gods for success in hunting, in marriage, and in battle.

The Kaw, Osage, Pawnee, and Wichita were living in Kansas when Europeans arrived there for the first time in 1541. A group led by the Spanish explorer Francisco Vásquez de Coronado reached Kansas while searching for Quivira, a mythical city of gold. When no gold was found, Coronado and his men left the area.

An Indian guide led
Coronado and his
soldiers through what is
now Kansas.

21

Horses and the Great Plains

Horses, brought to North America from Spain by explorers in the 1600s, changed the lifestyles of many Native Americans. On horseback, Indians were able to travel great distances in short periods of time, carrying their belongings with them.

During the 1600s, horses brought more Indians to Kansas. The Arapaho, Cheyenne, and Comanche were among the many tribes that rode on horseback from the north and the south onto the Great Plains. These Indians probably left their homelands in search of food or to escape their enemies.

Probably most important was that horses changed the way the Plains Indians hunted. Instead of stalking their prey on foot, hunters could ride alongside a herd of buffalo. Some groups of Plains Indians left their crops and villages to follow buffalo westward across the Great Plains.

French explorers and settlers arrived in the Kansas area during the 1600s and 1700s. Many of the French were fur trappers who captured beaver and other animals. The furs of these animals were sold to Europe to be made into fashionable hats and coats.

Before long, the French claimed a large area of what is now the central United States. They called their territory Louisiana. In 1803 France sold Louisiana to the newly formed United States. This deal, called the Louisiana Purchase, included the area that is now Kansas.

Meriwether Lewis

William Clark

The U.S. government was eager to map the land it had bought. Two army officers, Captain Meriwether Lewis and Lieutenant William Clark, were chosen to lead the mapping expedition. They passed through Kansas in June of 1804.

Lewis and Clark were not impressed by what they saw in Kansas. They thought the large expanse of dry grassland was of little use to the United States. Explorers who arrived later also thought the area was unfit for settlement.

Government officials agreed with the explorers but still had plans for the area. Many Native Americans on the East Coast had been forced off their homelands by European settlers, and the U.S. government had promised to give the Indians land in another area. In 1830 about 30 eastern tribes were ordered to move to Kansas.

Few trees and miles of open prairie greeted Lewis and Clark when they passed through Kansas in 1804.

At about the same time, large numbers of pioneers were heading west, looking for land on which to plant crops and raise livestock. Traveling on paths such as the Oregon and Santa Fe trails, these people only crossed through Kansas, which still belonged to the Indians.

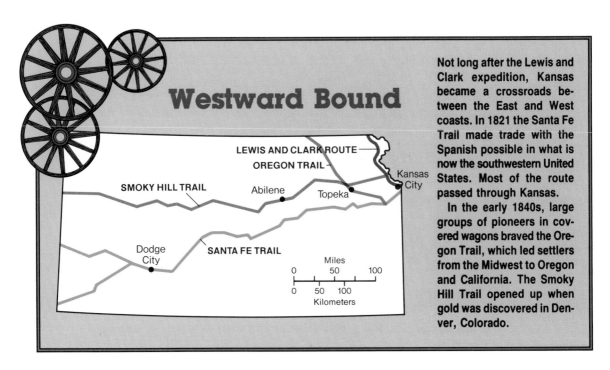

Westward Bound

LEWIS AND CLARK ROUTE
OREGON TRAIL
SMOKY HILL TRAIL
Abilene
Topeka
Kansas City
Dodge City
SANTA FE TRAIL

Miles
0   50   100
0   50   100
Kilometers

Not long after the Lewis and Clark expedition, Kansas became a crossroads between the East and West coasts. In 1821 the Santa Fe Trail made trade with the Spanish possible in what is now the southwestern United States. Most of the route passed through Kansas.

In the early 1840s, large groups of pioneers in covered wagons braved the Oregon Trail, which led settlers from the Midwest to Oregon and California. The Smoky Hill Trail opened up when gold was discovered in Denver, Colorado.

Travelers along the Oregon Trail cross a stream in eastern Kansas.

Fort Riley, near Junction City, was built in 1853 for the U.S. cavalry. In addition to being an army post, the fort served as a resting place for weary travelers and as a supply store for Indians and settlers.

In 1854 Congress passed the Kansas-Nebraska Act. This law made Kansas and Nebraska U.S. territories and opened them up to white settlers. The act also let Kansas and Nebraska decide whether to allow slavery within their borders.

During the 1850s, the United States was bitterly divided over slavery. The Northern states no longer wanted people to own slaves. The Southern states wanted to continue using slaves. After the Kansas-Nebraska Act was passed, the North and the South each tried to sway Kansas their way, throwing Kansas into a turmoil that would earn it the name Bleeding Kansas.

In 1855 Kansas held an election to decide whether the territory would support slavery. Citizens of Missouri, a neighboring slave state, poured into Kansas armed with guns. They beat up judges, voted illegally, and won control of the territory's government. After the crooked elections, the territory's new leaders created laws that ordered death for anyone who helped to free a slave.

People who favored slavery fought those who wanted to end it. Battles along the Kansas-Missouri border were especially violent. By 1858 antislavery forces in Kansas were strong enough to overthrow the territory's proslavery leaders, and by 1859 the new government

John Brown worked to make Kansas a free state. In 1856 he and his followers murdered five proslavery men, sparking more riots in Bleeding Kansas.

officials had outlawed slavery. Kansas was admitted to the Union on January 29, 1861, becoming the 34th state and the newest free, or nonslave, state.

The pictures on Kansas's flag tell some of the state's history. The covered wagons represent the journeys of the pioneers. The farmer, the plowed field, and the barn stand for agriculture. The 34 stars are for Kansas, the 34th state. And the Latin words *Ad Astra per Aspera* (To the Stars through Difficulties) refer to Kansas's troubled times before becoming a state.

Only a few months after Kansas became a state, the Civil War (1861–1865) began. The Southern states withdrew from the Union and formed the Confederate States, a separate country that allowed slavery. When Union troops were sent into the South to stop the Confederates, fighting broke out.

Few Civil War battles took place in Kansas, but thousands of Kansans lost their lives fighting for the Union army. Many of the state's soldiers fought in famous battles outside of Kansas. Most battles actually fought in the state occurred near the end of the war when Confederate, or Southern, troops stormed through eastern Kansas.

Quantrill Raid

Only a few battles were fought in Kansas during the Civil War. One was the Quantrill raid of 1863. William Clarke Quantrill lived in Lawrence, Kansas. For a time, he earned a living by stealing black slaves and then returning them to their owners for a reward. When the Civil War started, Quantrill joined the Southern, or Confederate, army.

In August 1863, Quantrill led a group of soldiers in an attack on the town of Lawrence. The soldiers burned most of the town and killed about 150 people, most of whom were not soldiers. Horrified, Confederate leaders arrested Quantrill for murder, but he escaped. Union troops found and executed Quantrill shortly after the Civil War ended.

After the Civil War, thousands of new settlers arrived in Kansas. Many came because of the Homestead Act, which offered 160 acres (65 hectares) of free land to anyone who was over the age of 21 and the head of a family. Congress passed this law to encourage settlement in the thinly populated western states, which included Kansas. Most of these **homesteaders** were taking a once-in-a-lifetime opportunity to be able to own land.

Homesteaders in Kansas faced many hardships. Surface water was limited, so settlers had to dig deep wells to bring water up from under the ground. Because few trees grew in Kansas, wood was

Soddies, or houses made of sod, kept early pioneers warm in the winter and cool in the summer.

scarce, and settlers had to build houses out of sod. To fuel fires for cooking and heating, homesteaders used prairie grass, sunflower stalks, buffalo chips, and even corncobs.

During the late 1860s, railroad companies began laying tracks across the United States. Cowboys

During the late 1800s, cowboys drove herds of Texas long-horned cattle through the streets of Dodge City.

and their trail bosses drove cattle from Texas to train stations in the Midwest, where the livestock could be transported to markets in the East. Several trails used by the cowboys ended in Kansas at Abilene and Dodge City. Before long, these two cow towns became bustling centers for trading and shipping cattle.

The Wild West

Wild Bill

Dodge City, 1880s

Brawling and drinking cowboys, who wanted to celebrate after weeks on the long, dry cattle trails, streamed through Kansas's cow towns. The cowboys gambled in the local saloons and sometimes even shot one another in the streets. Wyatt Earp *(top center)*, James "Wild Bill" Hickok, and William "Bat" Masterson *(bottom right)* were among the lawmen who were called in to stop the violence in Kansas, a state that belonged to the Wild West.

A Mennonite farm

Most Kansans, however, were farmers. These people, called sodbusters, cut down prairie grass, replacing it with crops. But raising crops was difficult. With frequent droughts in the area, farmers never seemed to have enough water for their fields.

In the 1870s, a Russian religious group called the Mennonites arrived in Kansas. Each settler carried a packet of wheat called Turkey Red. The wheat thrived in the dry fields of Kansas, and the state soon earned its title the Breadbasket of America.

More and more pioneers moved to Kansas and forced the Indians off the land. Bloody battles broke out between Native Americans and U.S. soldiers. After years of struggling, many of the Indians agreed to leave their homelands and move south to Oklahoma.

35

A farmer in Kansas stood on a ladder to show off his healthy corn crop.

The new settlers now had plenty of land on which to grow crops, and, as methods of farming improved, farmers were able to increase their crop yields. From the late 1800s to the 1920s, farmers went from using plows pulled by oxen and horses to using tractors with engines. Tractors could complete the work more quickly than plows could, and farmers had time to break more land. The state's crops were so abundant that other states depended on buying extra wheat from Kansas.

The state nearly lost its ability to feed the nation during the Great Depression of the 1930s. People throughout the United States had little money, so farmers had to sell their crops at low prices. Banks closed and people lost their savings. Many Kansans, along with other Americans, found themselves out of work.

The Breadbasket of America suffered even more when a long drought settled into the Midwest. With little or no rainfall, farmland dried up and crops died. Strong winds cut across Kansas, stripping farmland of its fertile soil. Wind

During the 1930s, dust clouds filled the air and blocked out the sun.

carried the soil in clouds of dust that coated everything in their paths. Southwestern Kansas became part of the **Dust Bowl,** an area of the Great Plains that experienced intense dust storms throughout the 1930s.

As the Depression and the dust storms eased in the late 1930s, Kansas slowly recovered. A major boost to the state's economy came during World War II (1939–1945). Kansas was rich in oil and other minerals, as well as in natural gas and helium. All of these resources were needed to keep factories running while the United States was at war overseas.

More than 200,000 Kansans

Sometimes oil gushing from a well could not be controlled for days.

38

General Eisenhower was respected by U.S. soldiers in World War II.

fought in World War II, including General Dwight D. Eisenhower, who was raised in Abilene. After planning the invasion of Normandy, a successful military operation that led to the end of the war, Eisenhower gained worldwide attention. He was elected president of the United States in 1952 and served for eight years.

Timeline

8000 B.C.	Native Americans arrive in the area that is now Kansas
A.D. 1000	Indians begin growing crops in Kansas
1541	Francisco Vásquez de Coronado reaches Kansas
1803	Louisiana Purchase
1821	Santa Fe Trail is established
1854	Kansas-Nebraska Act
1861	Kansas becomes the 34th state
1870s	Russian Mennonites bring Turkey Red wheat to Kansas

Today Kansas is a state with many industries and cities as well as farms and rural areas. While the state continues to undergo droughts, Kansans have learned from these hardships. Some farmers now use irrigation to keep crops watered, and trees have been planted to hinder dust storms. Conserving soil and water for future generations is a goal throughout the state.

ansas's state capitol building in Topeka took 37 years to build. Construction began in
66 and ended in 1903.

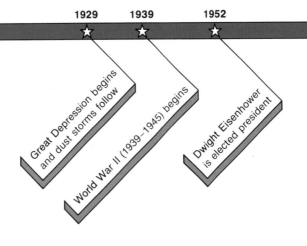

1929 — Great Depression begins and dust storms follow

1939 — World War II (1939–1945) begins

1952 — Dwight Eisenhower is elected president

Kansas prod... of winter w... the natio...

Farmers in irrigate, or ... **crops so the** **during drou...**

44

Living and Working in Kansas

The once dust-ridden cow towns of Kansas are now paved in concrete. Cars, not cows, travel down the streets of Abilene and Dodge City, and people live in houses of wood and brick instead of sod. But some things haven't changed. Many Kansans still make a living by working with wheat and beef, just as early settlers did.

Beef cattle graze on ranch land in Kansas.

Although fewer in number, farmers in Kansas still help to feed the nation. Each year, Kansans grow millions of tons of wheat—more than any other state. Many farmers plant the seeds of Turkey Red wheat, while others grow corn, hay, and soybeans.

Each year, farmers, ranchers, and modern-day cowboys in Kansas raise about six million head of cattle, which are later sold and butchered. Agriculture—farming and ranching—employs about 6 percent of working Kansans.

Other Kansans process the wheat and beef into food. Flour, which is made from wheat, tops the list of food products made in Kansas, a leading flour-milling state. Workers also pack meat and grind grain into food for livestock.

Kansas produces about 435 million bushels of wheat a year — more than any other state.

Production-line workers put the finishing touches on these airplanes.

Most of the light aircraft flown in the United States are made in Kansas. Wichita is well known for the large number of airplanes and helicopters it makes. Other products manufactured in the state are military missiles, railcars and train engines, trailers, and snowplows.

About one out of every six workers in Kansas has a job in a factory. But most Kansans have service jobs. In this type of work, people help other people or businesses in restaurants, banks, or hospitals. Other service workers sell the flour, beef, airplanes, and railcars made in the state.

Government jobs are service jobs too. Topeka, the capital of Kansas, is home to thousands of government workers. A major U.S. Army base, Fort Leavenworth, is located in the city of Leavenworth. This base, which also houses a prison, provides work for many Kansans.

More than half of Kansas's workers hold service jobs.

Minerals are found in most parts of Kansas, and the mining industry employs a small number of the state's workers. A huge salt deposit in Hutchinson yields nearly 45 million tons (41 million metric tons) of salt each year. Oil, which helps fuel U.S. industries, makes a lot of money for Kansas. Other resources include natural gas, coal, limestone, and helium, the gas that keeps balloons afloat.

The population of Kansas is nearly 2.5 million. People of European descent make up 91 percent of the state's population. About 5 percent of all Kansans are African Americans. Only about 15,000 Native Americans remain in Kansas. Asians and Hispanics are also a small part of the population.

About two-thirds of all Kansans live in urban areas. Wichita, Kansas City, and Topeka are the largest cities in the state, and all three are in the eastern half of Kansas. Western Kansas is mostly rural, but getting from town to town is easy. Kansas has more miles of highway than most other states.

Children play at a neighborhood swimming pool.

49

Fiddlers tune up their instruments to perform at the Svensk Hyllningsfest in Lindsborg. The festival, held every other year, honors Kansas's Swedish pioneers.

Both large and small cities in Kansas attract visitors. For western-art buffs, the Wichita Art Museum has a broad collection of western paintings and sculptures. In Lawrence, bug lovers make a beeline for the Snow Entomological Museum, which displays more than two million types of insects.

Anyone fascinated with cow towns and gunslingers will want to stop by Dodge City—Cowboy Capital of the World. In this colorful town, visitors can imagine what life was like during the time of Bat Masterson and the Wild West.

Front Street, Dodge City's main road in the 1870s, has been re-created at Boot Hill Museum.

An old train is on display in Lawrence.

Rodeos are held in many towns throughout Kansas.

Rodeos also help to keep the traditions of the Wild West alive. Throughout the state, crowds of people cheer as cowboys rope calves, ride bulls and bucking horses, and wrestle steers to the ground. Rodeos are held almost every weekend during the summer months. Horse racing and dog racing bring bettors to the Woodlands racing tracks in Kansas City.

The homes of two famous generals are found in Kansas. General George Armstrong Custer's home still stands at Fort Riley near

Junction City. Custer and his cavalry troops were killed by Sioux Indians in 1876 at the Battle of the Little Bighorn in Montana. A museum in Abilene houses the belongings of Dwight D. Eisenhower.

Kansas has nearly 200 lakes, which people use for fishing and swimming. Some other activities enjoyed in Kansas are hiking along part of the old Santa Fe Trail and camping on the prairie. Kansas, in addition to its cities and factories, still has plenty of wide-open countryside.

The University of Kansas Jayhawks draw large crowds at basketball games.

Protecting the Environment

Every spring, the people in central Kansas witness something spectacular. Throughout the season, millions of birds that have been flying nonstop for as long as 90 hours land at Cheyenne Bottoms, a 41,000-acre (16,592-hectare) **marshland** near the city of Great Bend. Here, the weary birds find the food, water, and shelter they need before continuing their journey northward.

When winter strikes, many northern birds leave for the warm, sunny South.

The birds are migrating, or moving from one region to another. **Migration** leads some birds southward in the fall. They leave their homes in Canada and the northern United States for places warm enough to supply food, such as berries and insects, during the winter. They return to their nesting areas in the spring, when food there is once again abundant.

Migrating birds follow the same path year after year. Some groups

Although different kinds of birds follow different paths, once a route is chosen by a certain type of bird, that path is traveled year after year. This chart shows the routes of the white-rumped sandpiper and the endangered whooping crane. Both birds make a stop at Cheyenne Bottoms.

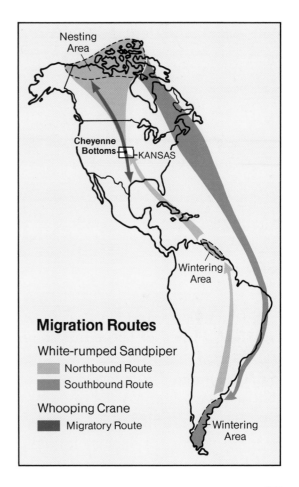

Migration Routes

White-rumped Sandpiper
- Northbound Route
- Southbound Route

Whooping Crane
- Migratory Route

of birds fly southward over the Atlantic Ocean in the fall. When they return in the spring, they follow a different route that takes them over the central United States. Many of these birds make Cheyenne Bottoms their first and only stop.

Pelicans

Lesser yellowlegs

At one time, Kansas had 12 large marshes. Only 4 of these marshes—Quivira, Jamestown, Slate Creek, and Cheyenne Bottoms—remain. The other wetlands dried up naturally or were drained of their water to make room for farms, homes, and businesses.

No one knows why, but migrating birds choose Cheyenne Bottoms as their stopover every spring. If Cheyenne Bottoms dried up, the millions of migrating birds that visit the marshland year after year would lose their place to feed and rest.

Cheyenne Bottoms provides food and nesting areas for nearly half of North America's north-bound shorebirds, or wading birds. It becomes a temporary home for 90 percent of certain bird populations, such as the white-rumped sandpiper, the long-billed dowitcher, and the endangered whooping crane. Waterfowl, including ducks and geese, abound.

The water in the Bottoms is generally shallow. The sun reaches the marsh's floor, encouraging plant growth. These plants are important foods for birds and other animals. By using their bills to dig deep into the mud floors, some birds also find beetles, leeches, snails, and worms. Water-fowl feast on fish and frogs. Cattails and other tall marsh plants provide food and shelter.

A scientist studies the eggs in a duck's nest in Cheyenne Bottoms.

Since the 1940s, Kansans have been keeping the water level in Cheyenne Bottoms desirable for the shorebirds and waterfowl that visit the marsh. Canals and **dikes** (artificial walls) control the flow of water among several pools within the marsh. When the Bottoms needs more water, it is pumped in from the Arkansas River and from nearby Walnut Creek. Without this extra supply of water, Cheyenne Bottoms would dry up during a drought.

Controlling the water level of the Bottoms, however, is more difficult than it might seem. People, farms, and businesses in Kansas also use the state's water supply, which is limited. When demands

In some places, the Arkansas River dries up for part of the year.

on water are heavy, the flow of the Arkansas River and of Walnut Creek stops or slows down and less water is available for Cheyenne Bottoms.

People have begun to study how much water Cheyenne Bottoms loses each year. By learning which areas of the marsh lose the most water and why, Kansans will be able to better manage its water supply.

Cheyenne Bottoms is one of the few remaining habitats in the United States for migrating birds. Controlling its water supply will benefit not only our fine-feathered friends but also the bird watchers in Great Bend.

Kansas's Famous People

Kirstie Alley (born 1955), from Wichita, Kansas, played the role of Rebecca Howe on the television series "Cheers" from 1987 to 1993. Alley has also starred in several films, including *Star Trek II*, *Look Who's Talking*, and *Sibling Rivalry*.

Hugh Beaumont (1909–1982) was better known as Ward Cleaver, father of Beaver on the television show "Leave It to Beaver," which aired from 1957 to 1963. Beaumont was born in Lawrence, Kansas.

▲ KIRSTIE
ALLEY

▲ HUGH BEAUMONT
(center right)

◀ DENNIS HOPPER

Dennis Hopper (born 1936), from Dodge City, is an actor and director. He has starred in several movies, including *Easy Rider* and *Hoosiers*.

Hattie McDaniel (1895–1952), born in Wichita, won an Oscar for best supporting actress for her role as Mammy in the 1939 film *Gone With the Wind*. She was the first African American to win an Academy Award.

Vivian Vance (1912–1979) was born in Cherryvale, Kansas. She became famous in the 1950s as Lucy's friend Ethel Mertz on the television show "I Love Lucy."

▲ HATTIE McDANIEL

▲ VIVIAN VANCE

John Steuart Curry (1897–1946) was a painter from Dunavant, Kansas. Some of his murals can be seen on the walls of the Kansas state capitol building.

Charlie "Yardbird" Parker (1920–1955), a Kansas City native, was a master of the jazz saxophone. He helped to create a fast style of jazz known as bebop. His saxophone playing greatly influenced later musicians.

▲ JOHN
CURRY

CHARLIE PARKER ▶

◀ WALTER JOHNSON

GALE ▶
SAYERS

ATHLETES

Walter Perry Johnson (1887–1946) was a baseball player born in Humboldt, Kansas. A pitcher and manager for the Washington Senators, Johnson was one of the first players to be named to the Baseball Hall of Fame.

Gale Sayers (born 1940), of Wichita, was a star running back for the Chicago Bears from 1965 to 1971. He was named to the Pro Football Hall of Fame in 1977.

Lynette Woodard (born 1959), a basketball player from Wichita, helped the U.S. women's basketball team win a gold medal in the 1984 Olympic Games. In 1983 Woodard became the first female member of the Harlem Globetrotters.

BUSINESS LEADERS

Walter Percy Chrysler (1875–1940) was born in Wamego, Kansas. A successful auto manufacturer, he was president of Buick Motor Company from 1916 to 1919 and founded the Chrysler Corporation in 1925.

Russell Stover (1888–1954) was born in Alton, Kansas. While working as a candy maker, he perfected the Eskimo Pie ice cream treat in 1921. Stover and his wife, Clara, later established Russell Stover Candies, now the largest boxed-candy company in the country.

▲ WALTER CHRYSLER

▲ RUSSELL STOVER

CRUSADER

Carry Amelia Nation (1846–1911) was a strong supporter of an old Kansas law banning the sale of alcohol. She was arrested several times for using a hatchet to smash up saloons, where drinks were sold illegally.

◀ CARRY NATION

CHARLES CURTIS ▶

POLITICIANS

Charles Curtis (1860–1936), a Kaw Indian from Topeka, served as the 31st vice president of the United States from 1929 to 1933 under Herbert Hoover. Curtis also held office in both the U.S. House of Representatives and the U.S. Senate.

Robert Dole (born 1923) comes from Russell, Kansas. Dole was a U.S. senator from 1969 to 1996 and was the Senate majority leader from 1981 to 1987 and from 1994 to 1996. Dole was the Republican nominee for U.S. president in 1996.

64

Dwight David Eisenhower (1890–1969), who grew up in Abilene, Kansas, became the 34th U.S. president in 1952 and held office for eight years. Eisenhower became a war hero after commanding a military operation in France that led to the end of World War II.

◀ AMELIA EARHART

DWIGHT ▶
EISENHOWER

SCIENTISTS & PIONEERS

Amelia Mary Earhart (1897–1937) was born in Atchison, Kansas. In 1932 Earhart became the first woman to fly solo across the Atlantic Ocean. In 1937 Earhart and her navigator disappeared in the Pacific while attempting to fly around the world.

Elmer Verner McCollum (1879–1967), a chemist and nutritionist, discovered vitamins A, B, D, and E in the early 1900s. McCollum was born in Fort Scott, Kansas.

WRITERS

Gwendolyn Brooks (born 1917), from Topeka, was the first African American author to win the Pulitzer Prize. She received the award in 1950 for her collection of poems entitled *Annie Allen*.

Gordon Parks (born 1912) is a well-known writer, photographer, and motion-picture producer and director. Parks, from Fort Scott, Kansas, won a Pulitzer Prize for photography in 1973.

GWENDOLYN BROOKS ▶

65

Facts-at-a-Glance

Nickname: Sunflower State
Song: "Home on the Range"
Motto: *Ad Astra per Aspera*
  (To the Stars through
  Difficulties)
Flower: sunflower
Tree: cottonwood
Bird: western meadowlark

Population: 2,477,574*
Rank in population, nationwide: 32nd
Area: 82,277 sq mi (213,098 sq km)
Rank in area, nationwide: 14th
Date and ranking of statehood:
  January 29, 1861, the 34th state
Capital: Topeka
Major cities (and populations*): Wichita
  (304,011), Kansas City (149,767), Topeka
  (119,883), Overland Park (111,790), Lawrence
  (65,608)
U.S. senators: 2
U.S. representatives: 5
Electoral votes: 7

*1990 census

Places to visit: Boot Hill Museum's Front Street in Dodge City, Dorothy's House in Liberal, Fort Leavenworth near Leavenworth, Fort Riley near Junction City, John Brown Memorial Park in Osawatomie, Kansas Cosmosphere and Space Center in Hutchinson

Annual events: International Pancake Race in Liberal (Feb./March), Flint Hills Rodeo in Strong City (June), World's Greatest Turtle Race and Fireworks Display in Ashland (July 4), Dodge City Days (July), St. Lucia Festival in Lindsborg (Dec.)

Natural resources: soil, natural gas, oil, salt, clays, coal, sand, gravel and stone

Agricultural products: beef, wheat, sorghum grain, hogs, corn, soybeans

Manufactured goods: transportation equipment, machinery, food products, chemicals, coal and petroleum products

ENDANGERED SPECIES
Mammals—black-footed ferret, gray myotis (bat)
Birds—bald eagle, whooping crane, peregrine falcon, least tern, black-capped vireo
Fish—Arkansas River shiner, pallid sturgeon, sicklefin chub, speckled chub
Amphibians—cave salamander, graybelly salamander, grotto salamander
Plants—Mead's milkweed, running buffalo clover, western prairie fringed orchid

WHERE KANSANS WORK
Services—55 percent
　(services includes jobs in trade; community, social, & personal services; finance, insurance, & real estate; transportation, communication, & utilities)
Government—19 percent
Manufacturing—15 percent
Agriculture—6 percent
Construction—4 percent
Mining—1 percent

MIN 1%
CONST 4%
AGR 6%
SERVICES 55%
MFG 15%
GOVT 19%

67

Abilene (AB-uh-leen)

Arkansas (AHR-kuhn-saw)
or (ahr-KAN-zuhs)

Cheyenne (shy-AN)

Coronado, Francisco Vásquez de
(kawr-uh-NAHD-oh, fran-SIHS-koh
BAHS-kayz day)

Eisenhower, Dwight (EYEZ-ihn-
how-ur, DWYT)

Mennonite (MEHN-uh-nyt)

Osage (oh-SAYJ)

Quivira (kih-VIHR-uh)

Topeka (tuh-PEE-kuh)

Wichita (WIHCH-uh-taw)

Glossary

dike A wall or dam built to keep a sea or river from overflowing.

drought A long period of extreme dryness due to lack of rain or snow.

Dust Bowl An area of the Great Plains region that suffered from long dry spells and severe dust storms especially during the 1930s.

glacier A large body of ice and snow that moves slowly over land.

homesteader A person who settled on and agreed to develop land that was given to him or her by the U.S. government under the Homestead Act of

1862. Most homesteading took place in the western United States between 1862 and 1900.

marshland A spongy wetland soaked with water for long periods of time. Marshes are usually treeless; grasses are the main form of vegetation found in marshes.

migration The movement of birds or other animals from one region or climate to another, usually for feeding or breeding.

prairie A large area of level or gently rolling grassy land with few trees.

reservoir A place where water is collected and stored for later use.

till A mixture of clay, sand, and gravel dragged along by a glacier and left behind when the ice melts.

Index

Acknowledgments:

Maryland Cartographics, Inc., pp. 2, 11; © 1992, Darrell Sampson, pp. 2–3, 25, 43, 49, 51, 52, 56, 70; Jack Lindstrom, p. 6; Kent and Donna Dannen, pp. 7, 12, 21, 42, 54–55; W. A. Banaszewski / Visuals Unlimited, pp. 8–9; G. Twiest / Visuals Unlimited, p. 10; Lynn M. Stone, pp. 13, 16, 17; Mike Smith, WeatherData, Incorporated, p. 15 (left, right); Kansas State Historical Society, Topeka, Kansas, pp. 18 (top left, top right, bottom), 31, 34 (top left, bottom), 63 (top left), 64 (bottom left, bottom right); Independent Picture Service, pp. 22–23, 24 (top, bottom), 65 (bottom); © The Detroit Institute of Arts, Founders Society Purchase, Dexter M. Ferry, Jr., Fund, p. 27; Wisconsin Veterans Museum, p. 28; National Archives, pp. 29, 34 (top center); Jeff Greenberg, p. 32; Library of Congress, p. 33; Kansas Collection, University of Kansas Libraries, pp. 34 (top right), 37, 38; Mennonite Library and Archives, North Newton, Kansas, p. 35; Joseph J. Pennell Collection, Kansas Collection, University of Kansas Libraries, p. 36; Dwight D. Eisenhower Library, pp. 39, 65 (top); John Charlton, Kansas Geological Survey, p. 41; James Blank / Root Resources, p. 44; Bruce Berg / Visuals Unlimited, p. 45; Cessna Aircraft Company, p. 46; Pizza Hut, p. 47; Lindsborg Chamber of Commerce, p. 50; Kansas Sports Information Office, p. 53; Jerg Kroener, p. 58 (left); Karl Grover, Kansas Department of Wildlife and Parks, p. 58 (right); Mike Blair, Kansas Department of Wildlife and Parks, p. 59; Stan Wood, Kansas Department of Wildlife and Parks, p. 60; Lucille Sukalo, p. 61; Hollywood Book & Poster Company, pp. 62 (top left, top right, bottom left, center, bottom right), 63 (top right); National Baseball Hall of Fame and Museum, Inc., p. 63 (bottom left); Chicago Bears, p. 63 (bottom right); Chrysler Corp., p. 64 (top left); Russell Stover Candies, p. 64 (top right); Schlesinger Library, p. 65 (center); Jean Matheny, p. 66; Doyen Salsig, p. 69.